MR MONKEY

AND THE MAGIC TRICKS

MR MONKEY

AND THE MAGIC TRICKS

Linda Chapman

Illustrated by Sam Hearn

Orion
Children's Books

First published in Great Britain in 2014
by Orion Children's Books
a division of the Orion Publishing Group Ltd
Orion House
5 Upper St Martin's Lane
London WC2H 9EA
An Hachette UK Company

1 3 5 7 9 10 8 6 4 2

The Orion Publishing Group's policy is to use papers that are
natural, renewable and recyclable products and made from wood
grown in sustainable forests. The logging and manufacturing
processes are expected to conform to the environmental
regulations of the country of origin.

ISBN 978 1 4440 0992 7

A catalogue record for this book
is available from the British Library.

Printed and bound in China

www.orionbooks.co.uk

*To Spike's own Mr Monkey,
who has a very mischievous
look in his eyes!*

Contents

Chapter One

This is Mr Monkey.

He looks like any other cuddly
toy. But Mr Monkey is magic –
yes, **magic**!

Mr Monkey belongs to Class Two. His magic is secret, and one thing's for sure, when Mr Monkey is around, exciting things start to happen!

"Who is going to take Mr
Monkey home and write his
diary this week?" Miss Preston
said to Class Two. "How about
you, Ben?"

Ben nodded. "Yes, please, Miss. You can come skateboarding with me, Mr Monkey!" he said.

It was Jack's birthday that day and in the afternoon he handed out a small bag of sweets to everyone.

Then Class Two put their chairs on their desks and Miss Preston said goodbye.

While his mum was talking in the playground, Ben sat down to eat his sweets.

"What've you got there, Ben?" It was a big boy, Ian, from Class Five.

"Just . . . just some sweets."

"Good. I like sweets." Ian grabbed the sweets and ran away laughing.

"Ben?" His mum came over.
"Are you all right?"

"Um, yes." Ben gulped.
"Let's go, Mum."

Chapter Two

Ben was quiet on the way home. When they got back, Ben took Mr Monkey upstairs.

He shut his bedroom door and sat on his bed. "I hate Ian," Ben said to himself. "He always takes things from me. I wish I could stop him but he's too big. I don't know what to do."

Mr Monkey sat up. "Never fear," he said. "Mr Monkey is here!"

Ben jumped so high he hit his head on the top of the bunk bed!

"You're . . . you're alive!"
Ben gasped.

"I know." Mr Monkey
hung down and waggled
his ears. "Hello."

Ben stared.

"It's all right," Mr Monkey said. "I understand. It always takes people a little while to get used to me."

Mr Monkey turned himself the right way up.

"You seem to have a problem," he said. "You can't let Ian keep taking your things."

"But how do I stop him?" Ben said. "He's bigger than me."

Mr Monkey scratched his head with his tail as he thought hard. "You know, I always think best when eating jam," he said.

"We've got some jam tarts downstairs," said Ben.

He came back a minute later holding one. "Is this OK?"

"Oh yes!" said Mr Monkey. "That's really got my brain turning. I know what you must do!"

"Next time Ian takes something, say to him, 'If you do that, you'll be sorry'."

Ben blinked. "He'll just laugh at me."

"Ah ha!" Mr Monkey tapped his nose. "But I have a Magic Masterplan and Mr Monkey's Magic Masterplans never fail!"

"Now." Mr Monkey gave Ben a hopeful look. "Are there any more jam tarts?"

Chapter Three

The school hall was loud and noisy at lunchtime the next day. Mr Miller, the headteacher, was on duty.

"Sit up!" he barked. "Elbows in!"

Ben opened his lunchbox. Just then, Ian appeared behind him.

"What have you got there?" he said.

He put his hand into Ben's lunchbox and scooped out Ben's favourite crisps and his chocolate bar.

Ben tried to remember what Mr Monkey had told him.

"If you do that, you'll be sorry!" he said.

"You'll be sorry if you don't shut up!" Ian said. He carried Ben's food back to the Class Five table and tipped it into his own lunchbox.

"Here, have some of my crisps," said Jack. The rest of Class Two all offered Ben something as well.

Suddenly they heard a shout.

"Worms!" Ian yelled.
"They're in my lunchbox!"
One of the girls at his table screamed. "There are earwigs too! Yuck!"

Everyone jumped to their feet.
"What on earth is going on?" shouted Mr Miller.

All the food Ian had stolen had turned into horrible bugs!

"Ian Macdonald," said Mr Miller crossly. "Will you please explain what is going on?"

"It wasn't me!" gasped Ian. "I didn't do it!"

"A likely story!" said Mr Miller. "How dare you bring these creatures into the lunch hall! Get rid of them and then go to my office!"

"But I haven't had any lunch," said Ian.

"There's your lunch. Just go!"
Mr Miller shouted.

Ian ran out of the room, his
face bright red.

"What happened?" hissed Halim.

"Someone must have played a trick on Ian!" Jack whispered.

Ben looked down at Mr Monkey. Mr Monkey winked.

Chapter Four

"Are you sure about this, Mr Monkey?" Ben whispered in the playground after school.

"I'm sure," Mr Monkey said.

Ben took a bag of sweets out of his school bag. He had brought them from home just as Mr Monkey had asked him to.

Ian ran up to him. "Give me those now!"

"No. They're mine," said Ben. He felt a bit braver than he had at lunchtime. "If you eat them, you'll be sorry."

"Oh yeah?" Ian emptied the bag into his mouth. "Says who?"

Ian started to cough. His hand went to his throat.

Miss Preston was nearby. "Are you all right, Ian?" she asked.

"Sweets . . . they taste . . . horrible." Ian started to spit them out.

But it was too late. Ben watched in surprise as bright spots popped out all over Ian's face!

"Oh my goodness!" Miss Preston said. "You really don't look very well. We'd better call your mum."

"What about football practice?" Ian cried.

"No football for you tonight," said Miss Preston, and she led him away across the playground.

"Mr Monkey and Ben two points, Ian a big fat zero," whispered Mr Monkey to Ben.

Chapter Five

On Saturday, Mr Monkey and
Ben had a great time going on
a bike ride. They didn't see Ian
at all.

"What are we doing today?"
Mr Monkey asked on Sunday.
"Can we go skateboarding?"

"I don't know. If we go to
the park, we might see Ian,"
Ben said.

Mr Monkey grinned. "And if
we do, it might be time for some
more **monkey magic!**"

Ian was playing with his friends near the skateboard ramps when Ben and Mr Monkey got to the park. The spots had gone from his face.

Ian left his friends and came over. "Give me your skateboard," he said.

Ben shook his head. Mr Monkey nudged him. "If you take it, you'll be sorry!" said Ben.

Ian hesitated.

"Let's go, Ian," his friends called.

"Coming!" said Ian. He pushed Ben off his skateboard, jumped on to it and started to skate towards his friends.

Then something amazing happened! The skateboard grew furry ears, a little tail and a row of sharp white teeth! It sped across the park with Ian.

"What's going on?" Ian yelled.

The skateboard whizzed up a ramp. Ian's arms waved round and he crashed to the ground.

"Great skating, Ian – not!" His friends laughed and left the park.

Ian sat up. The skateboard
wheeled round to face him.
"What . . . what's happening?"
Ian said.

The skateboard growled.

"Argh!" Ian jumped to his feet.
"It's horrible!"

"Not as horrible as you!"
said Ben.

The skateboard chased Ian
around the park.

"Make it stop, Ben! Please!"
Ian begged.

"Only if you stop taking my things," said Ben.

"I will! I promise!" Ian said. "I'm sorry I've been mean to you."

Mr Monkey pulled Ben's sleeve. "This is important, Ben. Say a spell. Make him think you can do magic."

Ben held out his hands and quickly made something up:

"Abracadabra, iggledytree,
Stop chasing Ian, he's said sorry!"

The skateboard turned back to normal. Ian stared. "How did you do that?"

"Oh, just a bit of magic," said Ben, with a grin. "You mustn't tell anyone though."

"I won't," Ian said. "And I promise I won't take your things any more either. I'll see you at school."

"See you there," said Ben. He wasn't scared of Ian at all now.

Ian hurried away.

Mr Monkey winked at Ben. "Stage Three of the **Mr Monkey Masterplan** complete!" he said.

Chapter Six

Ian didn't do anything horrid to Ben all week.

Mr Monkey told Ben to whisper, "You'll be sorry!" if he did start being mean again, but it seemed as if Ian really had learned his lesson.

When the time came for Ben to give Mr Monkey back, he took him into the cloakroom and gave him a hug.

"I'll miss you, Mr Monkey," he whispered. "Thanks for helping me."

Mr Monkey smiled. "I had more fun than a chimp in a roomful of bananas."

Miss Preston came into the cloakroom. "Ah, Ben. There you are. Come and share your Monkey Diary with the class and then I can choose someone else to take Mr Monkey home."

"I haven't written that much, Miss," said Ben.

"Don't worry," said Miss Preston. "The important thing is that you had fun together."

Ben grinned at Mr Monkey. "Oh yes, we **really** did!"

We went skateboarding.
We saw Ian from
Class 5. I had fun.

I hope Mr Monkey enjoyed his
skateboarding, Ben. I
think he'd be very good at it.

He is!